ISLAND Santa

SHERYL McFARLANE & SHEENA LOTT

CHILDREN'S HEALTH FOUNDATION OF VANCOUVER ISLAND

(formerly Queen Alexandra Foundation for Children)

Edited by Ann Featherstone.
Book design by Lara Minja, Lime Design Inc.
Upgrade to hard cover sponsored by Friesens Corporation.

Library and Archives Canada Cataloguing in Publication

McFarlane, Sheryl, 1954–
     Island Santa / Sheryl McFarlane ; Sheena Lott, illustrations.

ISBN 978-0-9880536-0-1

     I. Lott, Sheena, 1950– II. Queen Alexandra Foundation for Children (B.C.) III. Title.

PS8575.F39I75 2012   jC813'.54   C2012-902977-7

Printed in Canada

JENEECE PLACE
Caring for families

children's
HEALTH FOUNDATION
OF VANCOUVER ISLAND

For those
who generously give of themselves
to make their communities a better place;
and for my family,
who makes me a better person

⌐ S M

For Sophia and Adela,
and the families and supporters
of Jeneece Place

⌐ S L

"When's Santa coming to the island?"
Sophie asks a million times a day.

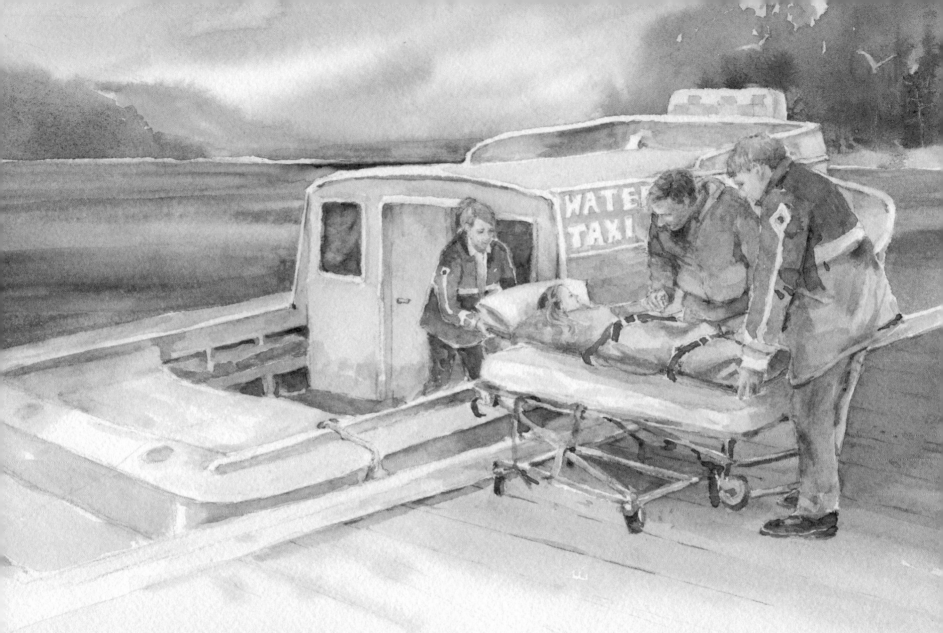

One day she doesn't ask, and deep down
I know she's sick again. A water taxi takes her
and Dad to the hospital in the city. Gran puts
an arm around my shoulder.

The whole island turns up for the Santa boat.
Hot chocolate and excitement keep us warm.
Last year Sophie was the one to see him first
and shout, "He's here!" But not this year.

Christmas carols float across the water. I stand in line with Gran, missing Dad and Sophie.

"Don't worry, Sam. You'll see them soon."

Gran takes me to meet the skipper of Santa's boat.
"Sorry to hear that Sophie won't be home for
Christmas," he says.
My tongue ties itself in knots, so I just nod.

"I told your gran I can get you to your dad and sister in time for Christmas."

I can't stop grinning. I feel like cartwheeling across the dock.

"But...," he continues, freezing the grin on my face, "...we have deliveries at a dozen ports of call. Can I count on you to help?"

"Yes, sir," I breathe. *I'm coming Sophie. I'm coming.*

My job is sorting presents for each stop—dolls, books, toy trucks, and puppets. An elf gives me a lesson in making balloon animals.

One island has a cool old fire truck waiting to take Santa to the hall.

The hall bursts with excitement. The line to Santa snakes through it all. I make a balloon dog for someone's little sister. It's crooked, but she doesn't mind.

After that, I have my own lineup.

Another island and another bay...
Our hands stiffen from the cold.
   Santa doles out presents, chuckles
when his stomach is poked, and listens.
   One girl asks to have a baby brother.
A boy wants a teddy for his sister, who
is home with the flu.

We motor through a swirling sea of white,
past ghost islands. We steer into the sheltered
waters of a narrow harbor. It's our last
delivery before we can fall into our berths
and sleep.

I wake up to a gale. Our boat is a roller coaster. Waves break across the bow.

Will I ever see my family again?

We pitch and shudder through high seas until we find shelter in the lee of an island cove. Half of Santa's helpers are seasick green.

An audience of seals watches us fix our tattered decorations.

The wind finally dies. A rising tide helps us make up time. The skipper steers past sandstone cliffs and caves the sea has carved into strange shapes. We slow to a crawl in open water.

"It's a bit tricky here," the first mate says. "Danger Reefs is to starboard and Miami Islet is to port."

"This is nothing like the Miami that Dad took us to!"

He laughs. "It's named for a ship that sank. No worries, Son. The skipper knows every inch of these waters."

Once safely past, we round a headland and anchor at the mouth of a shallow bay. Motorboats pick us up, and we hop out a few feet from shore. It's a good thing we're wearing rubber boots!

A bonfire welcomes us. We leave behind presents and happy faces.

Our pile of presents dwindles with each stop. We pass big and small islands and steer clear of hidden reefs and rocks. "Transients fifteen degrees to starboard!" someone shouts. All I see are whitecaps. Then they surface. Orcas. They blow. Disappear. And surface again.

It's dark by the time we reach the
lighthouse. They must have worried
that we wouldn't show.

I can't wait to see Sophie and my dad, but
a little piece of me doesn't want this trip
to end.

At the dock a taxi is waiting to take me
to my dad. I walk through grand double
doors into a living room with a totem pole
reaching for the sky. Dad comes running.
He lifts me off the floor and wraps me
in a bear hug.

I have a present from Santa, a slightly lopsided balloon dog, and a story that I can hardly wait to tell my sister.

The Story Behind ISLAND SANTA

Island Santa was inspired by the dedication of two people who never had the opportunity to meet. Although separated by generations, Jeneece Edroff and Kaare Norgaard (1916–2005) shared a vision to better the lives of children and families.

JENEECE EDROFF, a remarkable young woman from Vancouver Island, refused to let a painful and often crippling disease hold her back. At seven, she held a penny drive for Variety, the Children's Charity, and raised $164. By the time Jeneece was sixteen, she'd raised $1.5 million for Variety. But Vancouver Island's "Penny Girl" and the recipient of the Order of British Columbia didn't stop there. She dreamed of building a home away from home for island families like hers who had to travel to Victoria for medical care. In January of 2012, with the major assistance of the Queen Alexandra Foundation for Children, the Norgaard Foundation, TELUS, and a host of community service groups, corporations, and dozens of in-kind donations, Jeneece's dream came true with the opening of Jeneece Place.

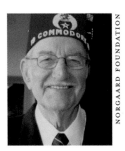

KAARE NORGAARD would have applauded Jeneece's determination and her community-minded goals. While he and his wife Bernice had no children of their own, each December Kaare transformed his ship, the *Blue Fjord*, into a floating sleigh that delivered thousands of Christmas gifts to coastal children who might otherwise have done without. In 1989, the successful businessman set up the Norgaard Foundation to better the lives of children and families. The Queen Alexandra Foundation for Children (now the Children's Health Foundation of Vancouver Island) and numerous charities have all benefited from Norgaard's generosity. ✴

Jeneece Place

JENEECE PLACE is a ten-bedroom, family-focused facility mere steps away from Victoria General Hospital on Vancouver Island. It's truly a home away from home for island families who must leave their communities to go to Victoria for medical treatment. It boasts a cozy living room that features a West Coast totem pole, a communal kitchen, dining area, games room, media and art rooms, and a garden and outdoor play area.

Visit jeneeceplace.org and childrenshealthvi.org for more information. ✳

LLOYD MILDON

SHERYL MCFARLANE is the author of more than a dozen books for children, including the multi-award winning picture book *Waiting for the Whales* and *Jessie's Island* with illustrator Sheena Lott. Her most recent title, *The Smell of Paint*, was awarded the Moonbeam Award for Young Adult Fiction in the U.S., and was a Canadian Children's Book Centre Best Book of the Year. Sheryl was brought up in Arizona but has made the West Coast her home for the past thirty years. ✳

SHEENA LOTT is an accomplished gallery artist and children's books illustrator who has published nine picture books, including Sheryl McFarlane's *Jessie's Island*, *Midnight in the Mountains* by Julie Lawson, and the perennial bestseller *Salmon Forest* by David Suzuki and Sarah Ellis. She has won many awards for her work, including the Myfanwy Spencer Pavelic Award. Born in Glasgow, Scotland, Sheena lives in North Saanich, Vancouver Island. ✳